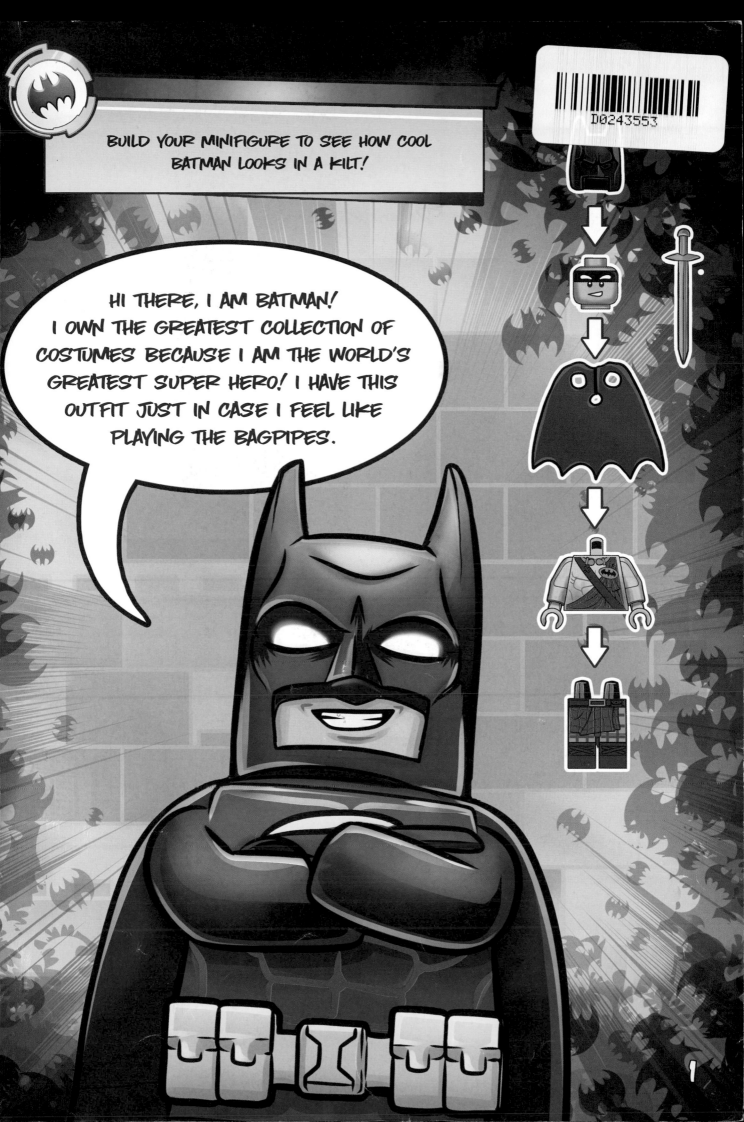

HERE COMES CHAOS!

THE ROGUE VILLAINS HAVE SET OUT TO CONQUER GOTHAM CITY. THEY ARE READY TO TAKE CONTROL OF THE CITY ... LEAVING NO BRICKS STANDING!

WE'RE THE BADDEST VILLAINS AROUND, AND WE STARTED OUR TAKEOVER BY RUINING OUR REFLECTION. CAN YOU SPOT 7 DIFFERENCES?

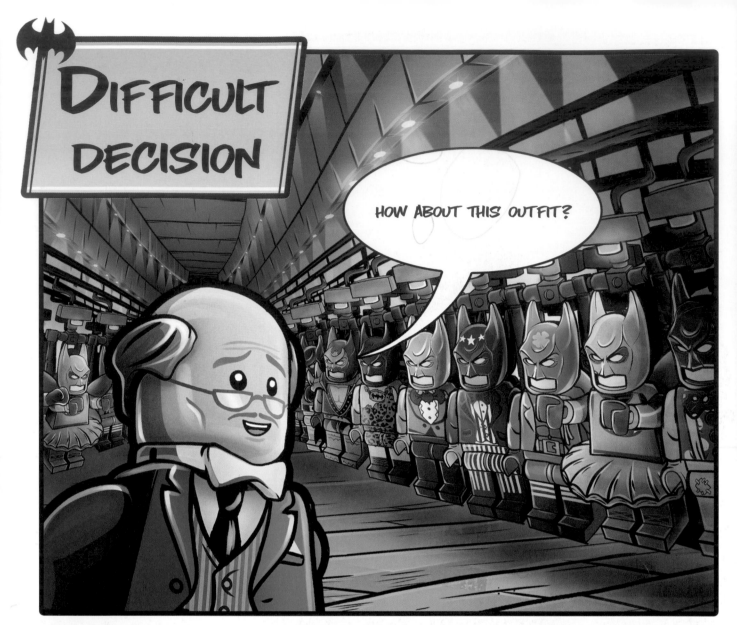

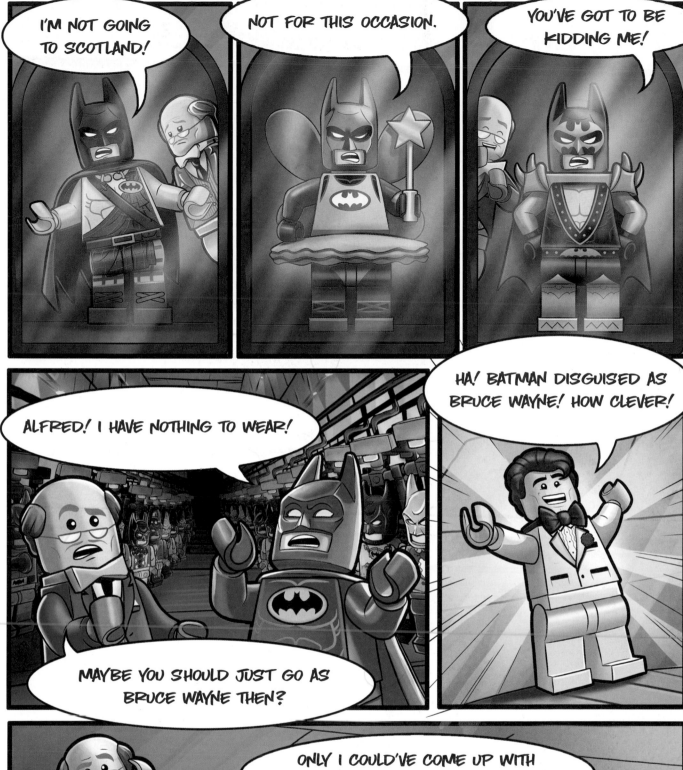

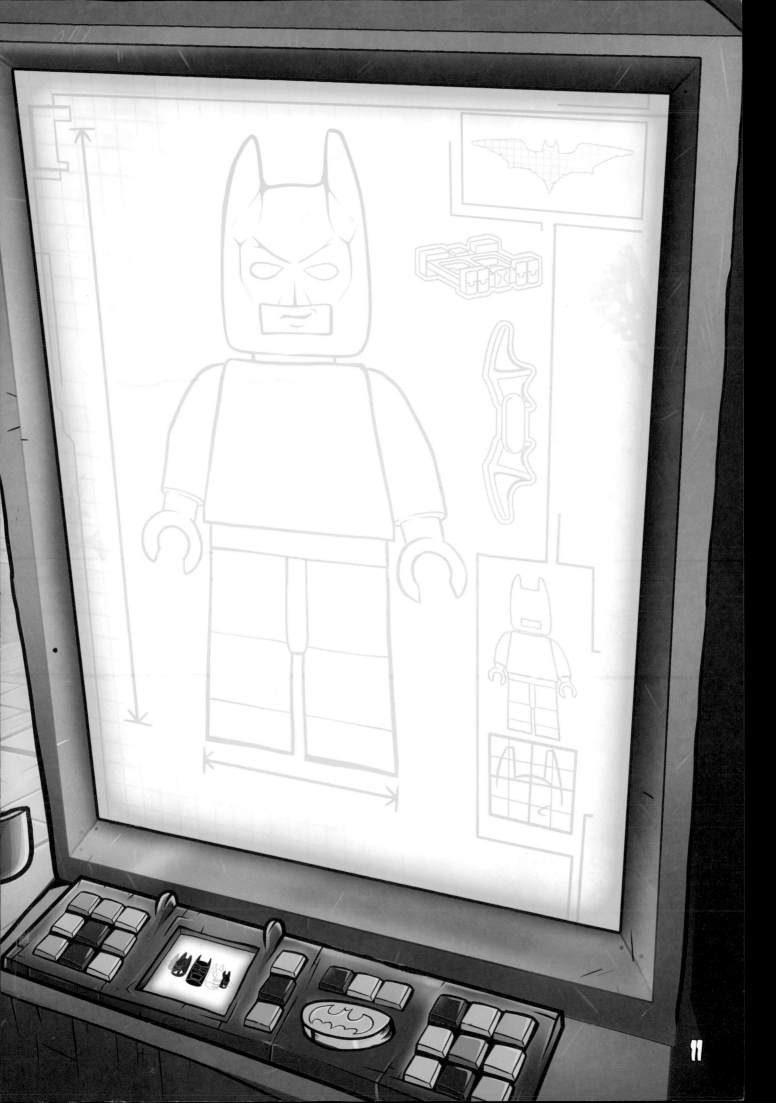

HEE HEE ... I CAN SEE THAT YOU'RE SPEECHLESS! I KNOW, IT'S AWESOME ... JUST LIKE ME!

BATMAN'S NEW TOY!

TWO OF THE SMALLER PICTURES DON'T MATCH THE LARGE SCUTTLER PICTURE. WHICH ONES ARE THEY?

CLAY'S PATH OF DESTRUCTION!

CLAYFACE LUNGES IN TO SMASH BATMAN! LIKE AN AVALANCHE,
HE TAKES DOWN EVERYONE IN HIS PATH!
WHICH VILLAINS ARE HIDING IN CLAYFACE'S BRICKS?

I'M GONNA CATCH YOU!

HEY! HELP ME FIND ROBIN,
BATGIRL AND COMMISSIONER
GORDON IN THIS CLAY CHAOS!

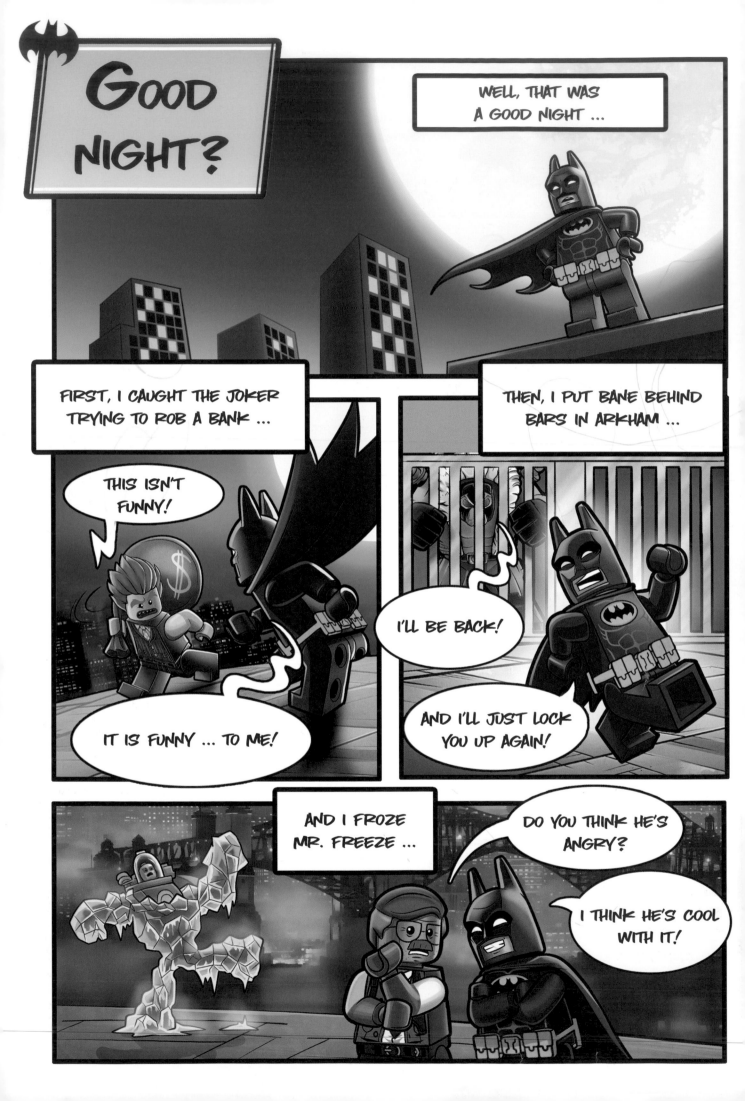

WHY BATMAN SHOULDN'T GO ON HOLIDAY ...

1. HE ALWAYS HAS PROBLEMS CHECKING IN.

2. HIS NEED OF HOME COMFORTS IS A LITTLE EXTREME.

3. HE NEVER STOPS THINKING ABOUT WORK.

4. HIS FANS FOLLOW HIM EVERYWHERE.

5. HE'S BORED OF ALWAYS BEING NAMED 'MR. BEACH' ... THERE'S NEVER ANY COMPETITION TO MAKE IT INTERESTING.

TOO EASY!

6. HE LIKES SURFING BUT ONLY ON HIS OWN TERMS.

TWO MORE WAVES AND YOU'RE FREE TO GO!

7. HE'S NOT USED TO SUNBATHING.

AARGH! ALFRED! WHAT HAPPENED TO ME?

8. ALTHOUGH HE WOULD NEVER ADMIT IT, HE REALLY LIKES SHOWING HIS HOLIDAY SNAPS TO OTHERS.

LOOK, THIS ONE'S REALLY GOOD, I'M NEXT TO A TREE. AND HERE I AM ON A CAROUSEL ...

IT'S BEEN TWO HOURS ... HOW MANY PICTURES IS IT POSSIBLE TO TAKE ON A TWO-DAY TRIP?

MISSING DETAILS

BATMAN HAS TAKEN A FEW PICTURES OF ROBIN AND BATGIRL. FIND THE COPIES OF EACH ONE AND SPOT ONE DIFFERENCE BETWEEN EACH PAIR.

I'M AFRAID SOMETHING'S NOT QUITE RIGHT HERE.

24

ALL LOCKED UP?

WELCOME TO ARKHAM ASYLUM! LOOK AT THE WANTED POSTERS AND CHECK THE INMATES TO SEE IF EVERYONE SHOWN HAS BEEN CAUGHT.

27

29

ANSWERS

P. 2-3

P. 4-5

P. 6-7

P. 12-13

P. 14-15

ANSWERS

P. 16-17

P. 18-19

P. 24-25

A-2, B-3, C-1

P. 26-27

ALL THE VILLAINS HAVE BEEN CAUGHT EXCEPT FOR THE JOKER.

P. 30